Jessica Souhami

Mrs McCool
and the
GIANT
Cúchulainn

An Irish Tale

Frances Lincoln

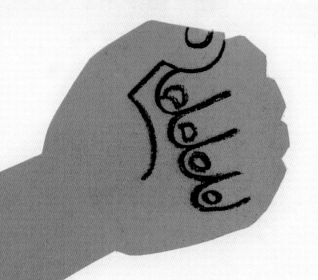

Long ago, there lived a giant called Cúchulainn.

My, but he was big and fierce and strong.

And what made him so strong?

He had a magic finger. And believe it or not,

all his strength was in that little finger.

Now Cúchulainn had fought all the other giants,

and squashed them flat. Well, all but one, and that

was Finn McCool.

"Where is that Finn McCool?" he said.

"When I find him... **POW! WHAM!**

Flat as a pancake he'll be. That'll prove I'm the

strongest giant in the world."

And off went Cúchulainn in search of Finn.

What was he like, this Finn McCool?

And where was he all this while?

Was he spoiling for a fight?

Well, that huge Finn was lying low and sucking his thumb!

But then, Finn's thumb was magic. When he sucked it Finn could see what would happen next. And he could see Cúchulainn coming to get him.

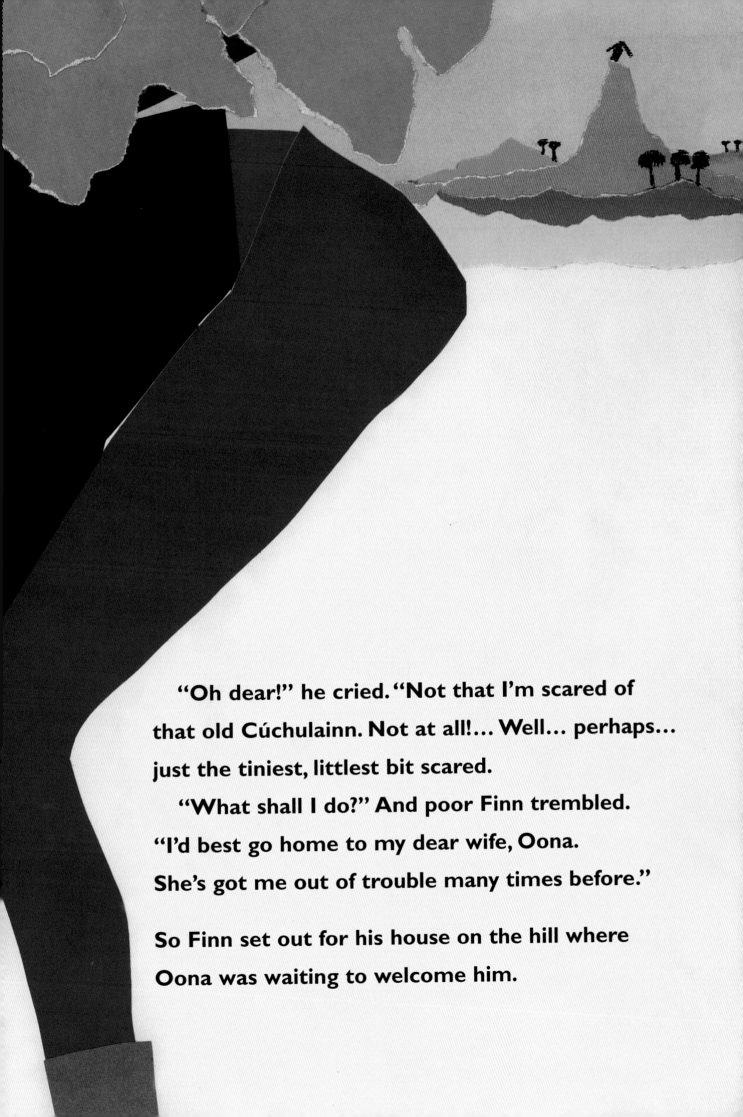

"Oh dear!" he cried. "Not that I'm scared of that old Cúchulainn. Not at all!... Well... perhaps... just the tiniest, littlest bit scared.

"What shall I do?" And poor Finn trembled. "I'd best go home to my dear wife, Oona. She's got me out of trouble many times before."

So Finn set out for his house on the hill where Oona was waiting to welcome him.

Finn told Oona all about Cúchulainn.

"Keep calm, Finn," she said. "I'll think of something. Just suck your magic thumb to see when Cúchulainn will arrive."

Finn sucked his thumb. **"Today, Oona!"** he called out. **"Today!"**

"Hmm," said Oona. "And when today?"

Finn sucked his thumb again. **"This afternoon!"**

"Hmm," said Oona. "And what time this afternoon?"

Finn sucked harder. **"At four o'clock!"**

"Four o'clock?" said Oona.

"That's TEA-TIME!"

She started to laugh. "I've such a plan, Finn!" she said.

And Oona set to work.

Oona started by making some bread.

She made enough dough for two, big round loaves.

She left one plain, but in the other she placed

an **iron griddle** – the iron griddle that

she usually heated on the fire to cook pancakes.

And when the two loaves came out of the oven

they looked exactly the same.

Then Oona hid Finn in a giant baby's cradle.

Well, all of him that would fit inside.

And she put a baby's bonnet on his head.

Then they waited for Cúchulainn.

They waited... and they waited...

And just as the clock was striking four, there was a great banging at the door.

"Do come in!" said brave Oona McCool.

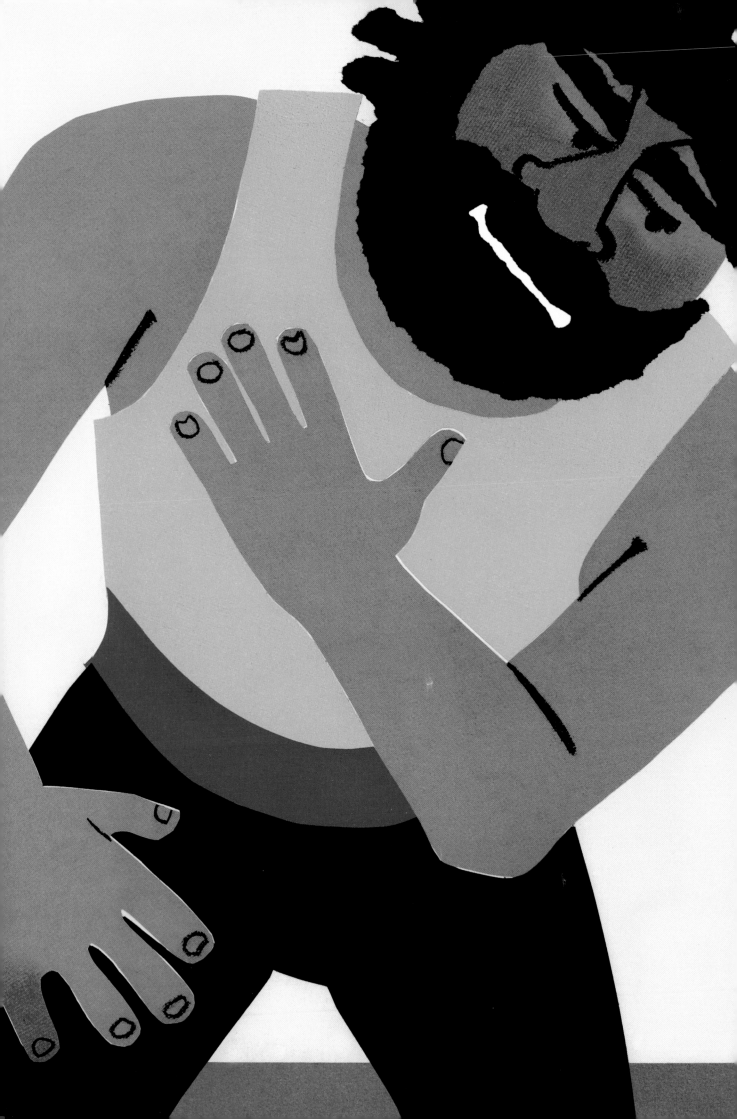

And in came the giant Cúchulainn.

"Is Finn McCool at home?" he boomed.

"No," said Oona calmly. "There's just me...
and the baby. Finn's out looking for some big silly
called Cúchulainn who wants to fight him.
Poor Cúchulainn! Finn'll make mincemeat of him!"

And she smiled up at Cúchulainn.

"BUT I'M CÚCHULAINN!"

"Bah!" said Oona scornfully, looking him up
and down. "You've not met my Finn! Well, you can
wait for him if you dare, and I'll brew some tea.
But first, will you do a small job for me? Will you lift
the house so I can sweep the dust from under it?
Finn does it every day."

What a storyteller that Oona was!

Cúchulainn was astonished.

"Well, if Finn can do it, so can I!" he said.

And he went outside.

Cúchulainn stretched out his brawny arms
and gripped the house.
He **heaved** and **shoved**,
and **grunted** and **groaned**,
and **grunted** and **shoved**,
and **heaved** and **groaned**.

And just as he felt he must burst, the house
began to move.

And Oona calmly swept the dust from under it
as if the house was lifted up every day.

"This Finn must be mighty strong," muttered
Cúchulainn.

Meanwhile Finn, hiding in the cradle, trembled
and shook from head to foot.

"Thank you, dear man," said Oona.
"Now if you'll just fill the kettle from the spring,
I'll make the tea."

Cúchulainn looked out.

"Where is the spring, Mrs McCool?" he asked.

"It's under that pebble," replied Oona pointing
to a huge boulder. "Finn lifts it to get water every day."

What a storyteller that Oona was!

Cúchulainn was astonished.

"That pebble's a mountain!" he said. "But if Finn can
do it, so can I!" He went down the hill and put his huge
shoulders to the boulder.

Cúchulainn **heaved** and **shoved**,
and **grunted** and **groaned**,
and **grunted** and **shoved**,
and **heaved** and **groaned**.

And just as he felt he must burst, the boulder
began to move.

Oona was as calm as if boulders were lifted
every day. But Cúchulainn, wearily filling the kettle,
was thinking, "Could this Finn be stronger than me?"

Meanwhile Finn, hiding in the cradle, trembled and
shook from head to foot.

At last, Cúchulainn sat down for tea...

"Do have one of my home-baked loaves,"
said Oona. And she gave Cúchulainn the loaf with the
griddle inside! He took a big bite.

"**Aaaaargh!**" he yelled.
"I can't eat this, Mrs McCool. It'll break all my teeth.
It's as hard as iron!"

"But it's Finn's favourite bread, Mr Cúchulainn,"
said Oona. "Finn and even the baby eat it every day."

What a storyteller that Oona was.

Just then, Finn called out, as if he really was a baby.
"Wah! Wah! Mammy! Hungry Mammy!"

"Oh see now, Mr Cúchulainn," said Oona trying
not to laugh. "You've woken the baby… Just give
him that other loaf, if you please."

And Cúchulainn did as she asked. But remember, this was a proper loaf. There was no griddle inside.

Finn ate the loaf in three bites!

"Yum-yum, Mammy!" he said. *"All gone!"*

Cúchulainn was astonished. If the baby could eat this bread, what could Finn do?

And should he stay to find out?

Just then, Finn sat up.

"GOODNESS!" exclaimed Cúchulainn.
"Look at the size of him! Look at that moustache!
If this is the baby, what must Finn be like?"

He moved to the door. "I really must be going,
Mrs McCool," he mumbled.

"Oh dear," said Oona calmly, "Finn will be sorry
to have missed you. Before you go, just see what
lovely teeth my baby's growing. Feel his little gums."

"Just to please you, Mrs McCool," said Cúchulainn.
"And then I'll be off."

Cúchulainn leaned over the cradle and put his little finger, his magic little finger into Finn's mouth. And guess what?

SNAP!
Finn bit it off!

**And with a whoosh,
Cúchulainn started to shrink.
He got tinier**
   and tinier,
     and teenier
       and teenier,
        and he ran right out of the house...
**...and he hopped and he jumped and he skipped
down the hill and he ran far away and was never,
ever seen again.**
   And as for Finn and Oona...

...They laughed and they laughed.

"Oona, my clever wife," said Finn. "You've saved me once again."

"It was nothing, dear Finn," said Oona. "Big is big. But brains are better!"

They danced and they danced... And if I'm not wrong, they are laughing and dancing still.

Mrs McCool and the Giant Cúchulainn copyright © Frances Lincoln Limited 2002

Text, illustrations and design copyright © Jessica Souhami and Paul McAlinden 2002

First published in Great Britain in 2002 by
Frances Lincoln Limited, 4 Torriano Mews
Torriano Avenue, London NW5 2RZ

British Library Cataloguing in Publication Data available on request

ISBN 0-7112-1822-6

Set in Gill Sans Bold

Printed in Singapore

1 3 5 7 9 8 6 4 2